DOVER · THRIFT · EDITIONS

Native American Songs and Poems

AN ANTHOLOGY

EDITED BY

BRIAN SWANN

DOVER PUBLICATIONS, INC.
Mineola, New York

DOVER THRIFT EDITIONS

GENERAL EDITOR: STANLEY APPELBAUM
EDITOR OF THIS VOLUME: STEVEN PALMÉ

Copyright

Published in Canada by General Publishing Company, Ltd., 30 Lesmill Road, Don Mills, Toronto, Ontario.
Published in the United Kingdom by Constable and Company, Ltd., 3 The Lanchesters, 162–164 Fulham Palace Road, London W6 9ER.

Bibliographical Note

Native American Songs and Poems: An Anthology is a new work, first published by Dover Publications, Inc., in 1996.

Library of Congress Cataloging-in-Publication Data

Native American songs and poems : an anthology / edited by Brian Swann.
     p.   cm. — (Dover thrift editions)
  Includes bibliographical references.
  ISBN 0-486-29450-1 (pbk.)
  1. American poetry—Indian authors. 2. Indians of North America—Songs and music—Texts. 3. Indian poetry—Translations into English. 4. Songs, American—Texts. I. Swann, Brian. II. Series.
PS591.I55N37 1996
811.008'0897—dc20   96-24331
                                            CIP

Manufactured in the United States of America
Dover Publications, Inc., 31 East 2nd Street, Mineola, N.Y. 11501

Introductory Note

Native American literature is all of a piece, from traditional songs and ceremonies that continue to this day (see, for example, "Havasupai Medicine Song") to the many poets who are now at the forefront of contemporary American literature. Like other poets, Native American poets write about all sorts of things, but tradition is a strong theme. So, when I invited participation in this venture, I wrote as follows: "I don't want to prescribe topics, but it might be a good idea to focus on the rich and complex theme of tradition and continuity, however you choose to treat it." Readers can discover for themselves how the poets interpreted this suggestion.

While most poets choose to write and publish in English, others compose in their native tongue and translate into English. They do this even though they feel some loss since, as the Navajo Rex Lee Jim wrote me, "writing poems in Navajo is like painting with the tip of a slashing whip." Ideally, poets writing in a native language would publish their poems in that language for, as Rex Lee Jim also said, "this would send a strong message that American Indian languages are alive and well, and active in the creation of American Indian literature."

I have adapted the traditional "song-poems" from the originals identified in the References at the back of the book. They were chosen almost arbitrarily and, since they are only a small sample, there is an unavoidable attenuation of theme and subject. Several of the contemporary poems have been previously published, and the works in which they first appeared are also listed in the References section. Those not listed have never been published before, appearing for the first time in this volume. For more songs and fuller notes, I refer the reader to the two volumes of mine from which I took the traditional songs, *Song of the Sky: Versions of Native American Song-Poems* (University of Massachusetts Press, 1993) and *Wearing the Morning Star: Native American Song-Poems* (Random House, 1996). For some more contemporary Native American poetry, see Duane Niatum's *Harper's Anthology of Twentieth-century Native American Poetry* (Harper and Row, 1988).

I would like to dedicate this book to the memory of Professor Willard Thorp, in whose graduate seminar at Princeton over thirty years ago my interest in American literature was kindled.

Contents

Song for Bringing a Child into the World[1]

[SEMINOLE]

let

the

child

be

born

circling around   You day-sun

you wrinkled skin   circling around

circling around   you daylight

you flecked with gray   circling around

circling around   you night sun

you wrinkled age   circling around

circling around   you poor body

---

[1]This song and the following "Song for the Dying" are sung by the medicine man or woman.

Song for the Dying

[SEMINOLE]

Come back
Before you get to the king-tree
Come back
Before you get to the peach-tree
Come back
Before you get to the line of fence
Come back
Before you get to the bushes
Come back
Before you get to the fork in the road
Come back
Before you get to the yard

Come back
Before you get to the door

Come back
Before you get to the fire

Come back
Before you get to the middle of the ladder

Come back

He-Hea Katzina Song[1]

[HOPI]

young corn-plants
in flower
a bean-patch
in blossom
under blue clouds
water will shine
after rain

Look
a throng of yellow flowers
yellow butterflies
chasing
one
another
through the bean-blossoms
blue butterflies
chasing
one
another

---

[1]*Katzinas* are intermediary deities, impersonated at ceremonies, who bring Hopi prayers to the gods.

Hymn of the Horse

[NAVAJO]

His voice   so grand
                        the turquoise horse of Johano-ai[1]

Rich blankets and hides
        hides of the buck, the beaver, buffalo and mountain lion
woven blankets
                        are spread
                                for his feet
Rich tips of flower-blossoms
                        Johano-ai
                                feeds him

spring water
                snow water
                        hail water
                                water from the world's four quarters
Now
        when he walks
                        grains of shining dust cloud him
        when he gallops
                        the sun's pollen
                                coats him in a mist

Now
        the herds of Johano-ai
                        increase for ever

---

[1]Johano-ai is the Navajo Supreme Being. He has five horses: one of turquoise, one of white shell, one of pearl shell, one of red shell and one of coal, and is said to ride the turquoise one when there are clear skies.

Deer Song[1]

[NAVAJO]

they start
          towards me
                    to my song
                              I am
                                   now
                              a glossy blackbird
from Black Mountain
                    on top
                              where the trail starts
                                        coming
                         now among flowers of all kinds
               coming
          now in among the dew
          now
     among the pollen
coming
     now
                         right there
                              the deer
                                        startled
                                             turning
                         left foot first
                              the male
                              right first
                         the female
          the quarry
          they
                    want me

---

[1]Hastyeyalti, god of sunrise and of game, makes hunting songs and hands them down to the Navajo.

Song from the Mountain Chant[1]

[NAVAJO]

the voice that makes the land lovely
again and again in sounds
among the dark clouds
the thunder's voice
the voice above
The voice that makes the land lovely

The voice that makes the land lovely
the voice below
the voice of the grasshopper
among the little plants
again and again it sounds
the voice that makes the land lovely

---

[1]The Mountain Chant is a nine-day ceremony intended to invoke unseen powers for curative purposes.

Song of the Earth

[NAVAJO]

The Earth is beautiful.
The Earth is beautiful.
The Earth is beautiful.

Below the East, the Earth, its face toward the East.
      The top of its head is beautiful.
      The soles of its feet are beautiful.
      Its feet, they are beautiful.
      Its legs, they are beautiful.
      Its body, it is beautiful.
      Its chest, its breast, its head feather,
      they are beautiful.

Below the West, the Sky, it is beautiful, its face toward the West.
      The top of its head is beautiful.
      The soles of its feet are beautiful.
      Its feet, they are beautiful.
      Its legs, they are beautiful.
      Its body, it is beautiful.
      Its chest, its breast, its head feather,
      they are beautiful.

Below the East, the Dawn, its face toward the East.
      The top of its head is beautiful.
      The soles of its feet are beautiful.
      Its feet, they are beautiful.
      Its legs, they are beautiful.
      Its body, it is beautiful.
      Its chest, its breast, its head feather,
      they are beautiful.

Below the West, the afterglow of sundown, its face toward the West,
  is beautiful.
Below the East, White Corn, its face toward the East,
  is beautiful.
Below the South, Blue Corn, its face toward the South,
  is beautiful.
Below the West, Yellow Corn, its face toward the West,
  is beautiful.
Below the North, Varicolored Corn, its face toward the North,
  is beautiful.

Below the East, Sahanahray, its face toward the East,
   is beautiful.
Below the West, Bekayhozhon,[1] its face toward the West,
   is beautiful.
Below the East, Corn Pollen, its face toward the East,
   is beautiful.
Below the West, the Corn Beetle, its face toward the West,
   is beautiful.

               The Earth is beautiful.
               The Earth is beautiful.
               The Earth is beautiful.

---

[1]Sahanahray and Bekayhozon are the holy spirits of the earth and sky.

Yaqui Song

[YAQUI]

Many pretty flowers, red, blue, and yellow.
  We say to the girls, "Let us go
    and walk among the flowers."
              The wind comes and sways the flowers.
      The girls are like that when they dance.
              Some are wide-open, large flowers, and
  some are tiny little flowers.

The birds love the sunshine and the starlight.

  The flowers smell sweet.

  The girls are sweeter than the flowers.

Quail Song

[PIMA]

The grey quails bunched tight together.
Above, Coyote trotted by.
    He stopped. He looked.

The blue quails ran and huddled together.
    Coyote looked at them,
        sideways.

Bear Song

[PIMA]

I am the Black Bear. Around me
    You see the clouds swirling.
I am the Black Bear. Around me
    You see the dew fall.

Havasupai Medicine Song[1]

[HAVASUPAI]

The land we were given
is right here,
right here.
Red rock
streaked with brown
shooting up high
all round our home.
Red rock
shooting up high
right here.
A spring will always be there
down at its foot.
From way back
it is ours.
Right down
the center of our land
a line moves,
bright blue-green.
This is what I'm thinking.
At the edge of the water
cattails appear,
bright blue-green,
all round the water.
This is what I'm thinking.
At the edge of the water
foam is forming,
swirling, swirling.
At the edge of the water
silt is being laid down
in ripples.
This is what I'm thinking.
Water skaters walk,
gliding, gliding.
This is what I'm thinking.
Water grasses growing,
bright blue-green
under the water,

---

[1]The song is received in a dream from a spirit and can be sung by someone who is sick and wants to cure himself. It describes Havasupai canyon in Arizona.

waving, waving.
This is what I'm thinking:
Under the water
tiny pebbles.
Flowing over them
the water we drink.
The water is gliding toward the north,
into the distance, beyond our sight.
That is what I'm thinking.
We have arrived here.
An illness.
I sit down,
I sing myself a song.
This is what I'm thinking:
A medicine spirit,
a healer,
I am the same.
An illness.
I sit down.
I sing myself a song.
The things I have named
I leave behind.
This is what I'm thinking.
We arrive there.
We are leaving the canyon.
Out on the rim
horses that are mine.
They roam there
at the junipers,
where the junipers are straight,
and low.
They are right there,
horses that are mine
are gathered there.
This is what I'm thinking.
Here we arrive, then
we swing back down,
moving back down the rocks,
white rocks streaked with brown.
Down at the foot
a spring will always be there,
a spring that heals,
it is right there.
My horses drink the water
that is there.

White rock streaked with brown
shooting up high
is right there.
There is my horse's trail,
zigzagging right down the center,
the color of dust.
It leads to
the source.
It is right here.
That is what I'm thinking.
And now we arrive
down in the canyon,
red rocks,
down in the canyon,
they are right here,
down in the canyon,
red rocks, low down,
they are right here.
Here I walk,
I go alone.
This is what I'm thinking.
Red rocks, streaked with brown,
shooting up high.
It is right here,
down at the foot,
red rocks, boulders
streaked with brown.
They are right here.
My illness is absorbed,
right here.
I will this to be.
I will this to be.

Arapaho Ghost Dance Songs[1]

[ARAPAHO]

I

How bright the moonlight
how bright the moonlight
as I ride in with my load of buffalo meat

II

My father did not recognize me.
Next time he saw me he said,
You are the child of a crow.

III

I am looking at my father
I am looking at him
     he is beginning to turn into a bird
        turning into a bird

IV

They say
the spirit army is approaching,
the spirit army is approaching,
the whole world is moving onward,
the whole world is moving onward.
See, everybody is standing, watching.
Everybody is standing, watching.

V

The whole world is coming,
a nation is coming, a nation is coming.
The Eagle has brought the message to the people.
The father says so, the father says so.
Over the whole earth they are coming.
The buffalo are coming, the buffalo are coming.
The Crow has brought the message to the people,
the father says so, the father says so.

---

[1]Songs come from the dancers' visions, describing experiences in the vision world. The Ghost Dance was intended to bring back pre-reservation days (see song V). The Crow of songs II and V is the messenger from the spirit world (as is the Eagle). In song VI the Messiah addresses his children. "Paiute Ghost Dance Song" contains the doctrine of the new earth that is approaching.

VI

My children, my children,
it is I who wear the morning star on my head.
It is I who wear the morning star on my head.
I show it to my children.
I show it to my children.

Paiute Ghost Dance Song

[PAIUTE]

Snowy earth
comes
swirling
ahead
of the whirlwind
ahead
of the whirlwind
snowy earth
swirling

Luiseño Songs of the Seasons[1]

[LUISEÑO]

I

The ant has his season;
he has opened his house.
   When the days grow warm he comes out.
The spider has her house and her hill.
   The butterfly has her enclosure.
The chipmunk and squirrel have their hollowed logs for acorns.
   It is time for the eagle to take off.
It will soon be time for the acorns to fall from the trees.

II

In the north the bison have their breeding grounds,
and the elk drops her young.
   In the east the the mountain sheep
and the horned toad have their young.
   In the south other animals give birth.
In the west the ocean is heaving,
   tossing its waves back and forth.
Here, at this place, the deer sheds his hair
   and the acorns grow fat.
the sky sheds, changing color,
   white clouds swept away.

III

The Milky Way lies stretched out on its back,
making a humming sound.

From the door of my house I recognize in the distance
Nahut, the stick used to beat Coyote, and Kashlapish,
   the ringing stones. I look up.

Look: Antares is rising,
      Altair is rising. The Milky Way,
         Venus is rising.

---

[1]These songs are part of the "Image Ceremony."

Six Dream Songs[1]

[WINTU]

I: You and I Shall Go

                              above
                    above
you and I shall go
                              you and I shall go
                    along the Milky Way
                         along the trail of flowers
you and I shall go
                    picking flowers on our way
you and I shall go

II: Minnow and Flowers

flowers droop
flowers rise back up
above
the place where
the minnow sleeps while
her fins move slowly
back & forward
forward
&
back

III: Sleep

Where will you and I sleep?
At the down-turned jagged rim of the sky you
& I will sleep.

---

[1]Dream Songs formed the chief feature of the Dream Dance Cult and were given in sleep by a dead friend or relative. The Land of the Dead is "above" and the Milky Way is the road the spirits travel to their final resting place.

IV: Dandelion Puffs

         above

      rise

    will   swaying

  of people   like women

The spirits

        while men dance,

     swaying with dandelion puffs

in their hands.

V: There Above

      spirits are wafted along the roof &

   at the Earthlodge of the South

 there above

There above

                   fall.

Flowers bend heavily on their stems.

VI: Strange Flowers

      Above

in the west, in the flat of the flowers

 strange flowers bloom,

   flowers with crests

bending to the east.

Two Newe Songs

[NEWE]

I

    Song Woman
sits beating the rhythm of her song.
    Song Woman
sits beating the rhythm of her song
there in a distant place,
next to her cousin, the water,
beating the rhythm of her song,
beating the rhythm of her song.

II

There, in a distant place, she sits in an arroyo.
There, in a distant place, she sits in an arroyo
        winnowing the pine nuts,
      by the red-rock-wooded place
        winnowing the pine nuts.

Song[1]

[NOOTKA]

You only achieve this with old age:
              I look like a sea-parrot
              with white patches
              on each side of my head.

Try to become old as fast as you can.
              I look so handsome.

---

[1]As the solo dancer sings, he holds up his hand as though it were a mirror.

Cradle Song

[HAIDA]

You
    where have you
        fallen
           from

              fallen

                You
             have been
        falling
      falling
   Have you
      fallen
        from the top
          of the salmon-
             berry bushes

          falling

             falling

In the Valley

[TSIMSHIAN]

As I sit here in the valley
all the heart has gone out of me.

I threw a stone at the blue grouse[1]
on the side of the mountain.

It hit her, and she flew off.
I re-wove the rotten fish-basket,

fixed it up for use again in the
foothills. But, sick at heart,

I have cut it to pieces. While
I was weaving another, a bat flew

right at me.[2] I will not do what
it orders, the small moth-spirit

that flew at me here in the valley.
Right here in the valley,

all the heart has gone out of me.

She Will Gather Roses[3]

[TSIMSHIAN]

This little girl
only born to
gather wild roses.
Only born to
shake the wild rice loose
with her little fingers.
Only to collect the sap
of young hemlocks

---

[1]The blue grouse is probably the woman the man has sent away.
[2]When a bat hits someone it means that person is about to die.
[3]A lullaby for girls.

in spring. This woman-
child was only born
to pick strawberries,
fill baskets with
blueberries, soapberries,
elderberries. This
little girl was
only born to
gather wild roses.

Utitia'q's Song[1]

[INUIT]

I am happy.
This is good.
There is nothing but ice all around.
That is good.
I am happy.
This is good.
For land we have slush.
That is good.
I am happy.
This is good.
When I do not know enough
It is good.
When I tire of being awake
I begin to wake.
It gives me joy.

---

[1]Utitia'q went adrift on the ice while sealing and only reached shore after a week of hardship.

Dance Song

[INUIT]

The animals are beautiful.
There is no song about it
since words are hard to find—
Seals on the ice down there—
When I found a few words
I fastened them to the music—
they left for their breathing holes—
The animals are beautiful.
There is no song about it
since words are hard to find—
Antlered caribou on the land over there—
When I found a few words
I fastened them to the music—
when it crossed the tundra over there—
The animals are beautiful.
There is no song about it
since words are hard to find—
Bearded seals on the ice down here—
When I found a few words
I fastened them to the music
when they left for their breathing holes.

Old Song of the Musk Ox People

[INUIT]

It is glorious
when the caribou herds leave the forests
and begin to wander northward.
They are on the alert for deep pitfalls in the snow,
the great herds from the forests,
when they spread out over the snow—
they are glorious!
It is glorious
when early summer's thin-coated caribou begin to wander;
when at Haningassoq, down there, over the promontories,
they mill back and forth looking for a crossing place.
It is glorious
when the great musk oxen
down there, glossy, black,
cluster in small groups
to face and watch the dogs.
When they bunch together like that
they are glorious!
The women down there are glorious
when they go visiting the houses in small flocks,
and the men down there suddenly feel
the need to boast and prove their manhood,
while the women try to catch them in a lie!
It is glorious
when the winter caribou with their thick coats
begin their trek back, in toward the forests.
They are glorious!
They look about anxiously for people.
When they are moving in toward the forests
they are glorious!
The enormous herds are glorious
when they begin to wander down there by the sea,
down by the beach.
The creaking whisper of hooves when they begin to wander around—
oh, it is glorious!

Delight in Nature

[INUIT]

Isn't it lovely,
the little river cutting through the gorge
when you approach it slowly
while trout are standing
behind stones in the stream?

Isn't it lovely,
the river's thick grass banks?
But I shall never again
meet Willow Twig, my dear friend
I long to see again.
Well, that's how it is.
The winding run
of the stream through the gorge
is lovely.

Isn't it lovely,
the bluish rocky island out there
when you approach it slowly?
What does it matter
that the blowing spirits of the air
stray over the rocks
because the island is lovely
when you approach it
at an easy pace
and haul it in?

Ptarmigan

[INUIT]

A small ptarmigan sat
in the middle of the plain
on top of a snowdrift.
Its eyelids were red
and its back streaked brown.
And right under its cute tail feathers
sat the sweetest little rump.

How to Write the Great American Indian Novel

Sherman Alexie   [SPOKANE / COEUR D'ALENE]

All of the Indians must have tragic features: tragic noses, eyes, and arms.
Their hands and fingers must be tragic when they reach for tragic food.

The hero must be a half-breed, half white and half Indian, preferably
from a horse culture. He should often weep alone. That is mandatory.

If the hero is an Indian woman, she is beautiful. She must be slender
and in love with a white man. But if she loves an Indian man

then he must be a half-breed, preferably from a horse culture.
If the Indian woman loves a white man, then he has to be so white

that we can see the blue veins running through his skin like rivers.
When the Indian woman steps out of her dress, the white man gasps

at the endless beauty of her brown skin. She should be compared to nature:
brown hills, mountains, fertile valleys, dewy grass, wind, and clear water.

If she is compared to murky water, however, then she must have a secret.
Indians always have secrets, which are carefully and slowly revealed.

Yet, Indian secrets can be disclosed suddenly, like a storm.
Indian men, of course, are storms. They should destroy the lives

of any white women who choose to love them. All white women love
Indian men. That is always the case. White women feign disgust

at the savage in blue jeans and t-shirt, but secretly lust after him.
White women dream about half-breed Indian men from horse cultures.

Indian men are horses, smelling wild and gamey. When the Indian man
unbuttons his pants, the white woman should think of topsoil.

There must be one murder, one suicide, one attempted rape.
Alcohol should be consumed. Cars must be driven at high speeds.

Indians must see visions. White people can have the same visions
if they are in love with Indians. If a white person loves an Indian

then the white person is Indian by proximity. White people must carry
an Indian deep inside themselves. Those interior Indians are half-breed

and obviously from horse cultures. If the interior Indian is male
then he must be a warrior, especially if he is inside a white man.

If the interior Indian is female, then she must be a healer, especially
if she is inside a white woman. Sometimes there are complications.

An Indian man can be hidden inside a white woman. An Indian woman
can be hidden inside a white man. In those rare instances,

everybody is a half-breed struggling to learn about their horse culture.
There must be redemption, of course, and sins must be forgiven.

For this, we need children. A white child and an Indian child, gender
not important, should express deep affection in a child-like way.

We should all be reminded that we are children. We should learn
about geometry: circles and squares, parallel lines and intersections.

In the Great American Indian novel, when it is finally written,
all of the white people will be Indians and all of the Indians will be ghosts.

Grandmother

Sherman Alexie

old crow of a woman in bonnet, sifting through the dump
salvaging those parts of the world
neither useless nor useful

she would be hours in the sweatlodge
come out naked and brilliant in the sun
steam rising off her body in winter
like a slow explosion of horses

she braided my sisters' hair with hands that smelled deep
roots buried in the earth
she told me the old stories

how time never mattered
when she died
they gave me her clock

Two Heart Clan

Duane Big Eagle   [OSAGE]

Two Hearts are always first
to send blankets and food to a sing.
Two Hearts know that stolen objects
always go back where they belong.
Two Hearts keep silent when they have
nothing to say, but gossip travels like an arrow.
Two Hearts stay up late at a 49 dance[1]
and wake up bleary-eyed with the sun.
Two Hearts bring venison at mid-winter
to the wind blown lodges of the elders.
Two Hearts die in heat-shimmering prairie grass
and are buried facing east
under piles of red rock.
Two Hearts raise the sun with their prayers
and call deaf-eared rain with gesture
old as rain itself.
Two Hearts never do what they're told
and their children grow up strongly steady reeds
impervious to wind.
Two Hearts camp under late summer cottonwoods;
their gray smoke lifts
soft white seed to the sky.
Two Hearts read the winter in a spider web
leaping against its anchoring strands
in the first cool wind of autumn.
A Two Heart life is the journey of a star
from blue evening through black night
to red dawns' horizon.
Two Hearts know we all must leave this world,
yet they laugh, they laugh, they laugh.

---

[1]A 49 dance is held after a regular powwow and can often last all night.

Inside Osage

Duane Big Eagle

The town crier's first bell sounds
calling dancers to get dressed
and head for the arbor.
Soon drums and singing
will float across these wide fields.
I sit for a moment
on a wood splitting stump
by the low concrete porch
and remember how the houses
are built practically on the ground,
and how the rivers and creeks
have their own distinct smells.
How it feels to be so far
from a main road
that you see fifty miles
across low hills and gullies
covered in prairie grass
rippling in a breeze
all the way from Nebraska.
Meadowlarks whistle sunlit melodies
and a single shrill hawk's shriek
arouses my heart.
Tourists may see gas stations, farms,
cattleguards across red dirt roads,
and asphalt highways
speeding through one street towns.
But if you look carefully,
you can find another land hidden here,
the invisible vertical to this horizontal world.
Rising up as a high school
in the middle of nowhere,
glimpsed in the blue flash of a thunderstorm,
it's an older land where war honors
are still being sung,
where cooking fires still send out
a warm invitation of good smells,
where eagle feathers stand upright
in fields of undisturbed snow.
I feel it at the dances,
on the evening of the third day
during the last songs,
when the circle of women singers
stand up from their chairs

and sing behind the men.
Drumsticks swing up like
beating wings of an eagle;
dancers circle, then face in to the singers
as a shimmering column
of sound and light
rises out of the drum
and races toward the sky.

Anza Borrego, 1995[1]

Kim Blaeser   [ANISHINAABE]

Grace wavers
like memory,
a fragile uncertainty.
The mapping
of ephemeral streams
on desert terrain,
witnessed
by faint marks
across the land,
read by faith.
The history of a wash
waiting
to be filled.

One surprise rain
colors rock and sand.
Desert rain
filling each crevice
of pain packed earth.
Waking scent
yucca and creosote,
teasing out
small blossoms.
Tiny rivulets
of freedom
trickle down,
run overflow
finding
ancient paths
washing them clean
of history's debris.

Palm oasis
hidden mid-mountain

[1]The Anza Borrego is a desert wilderness area in Southern California.

on rocky treks.
Shades of green and blue
amid dusty grays and browns.
Cool pools of grace
soothing.
A chimera
sighted
like silhouettes
of big horn sheep
on distant peaks.
Once a mirage
wavering
shimmering hope
in every hot sun
a trick of vision
or light
pursued to death
by every lost traveler.
But listen.
What they have never named
cannot claim
survived here
on roots
and cactus milk.
Jack rabbit terrain
cracked open in thirst,
Morteros,[2]
hollowed bellies of rocks,
fill now
with rain and memory.
Oh Kumeyaah and Cahuilla,[3]
Oh desert dwellers
of earth or spirit,
all ephemeral voices
of this America,
echo here.
Each hollow lie
of history
waits to be filled.
And now we send our words
to fall
like snow
in the desert.

---

[2]*Morteros* are hollowed portions of boulders used by native peoples for pounding and grinding seeds and pods.
    [3]The Kumeyaah (sometimes called Southern Dieguenos) and Cahuilla are tribes who inhabited the Anza Borrego area.

Ride the Turtle's Back

Beth Brant   [MOHAWK]

A woman grows hard and skinny.
She squeezes into small corners.
Her quick eyes uncover dust and cobwebs.
She reaches out
for flint and sparks fly in the air.
Flames turned loose on fields
burn down to bare seeds
we planted deep.

The corn is white and sweet.
Under its pale, perfect kernels
a rotting cob is betrayal.
It lies in our bloated stomachs.

I lie in Grandmother's bed
and dream the earth into a turtle.
She carries us slowly across the universe.
The sun warms us.
At night the stars do tricks.
The moon caresses us.

We are listening for the sounds of food.

Mother is giving birth, Grandmother says.
Corn whispers.

Earth groans with labor
turning corn yellow in the sun.

I lie in Grandmother's bed.

We listen.

Geese Flying over a Prison Sweat Lodge
Fox Lake, Wisconsin
Joseph Bruchac   [ABENAKI]

Inside an arch
like that of the sky,
(unlike that arch of mortared stone
with razor wire on top,
which we walk beneath
to find freedom within concrete)
inside the shell of the old turtle,
inside the body of our mother,
inside our memories
waiting to be born again
we hear the sound,
of flock after flock
their ancient calls
of welcome and question,
seeking relatives
after a winter's exile.

Hiss of water on stone,
and the cries of the geese
bark an answer,
their touch deep as bone,
speaking words never written
that always mean home.

The Owl

Joseph Bruchac

The Owl, that was the name they called me
as I went without sleep night after night
in that autumn of my twentieth year
as I walked the halls of a college fraternity.
Ko-ko-has Ko-ko-has Ko-ko-has

Sound in the forest of enemy feet
dark faces, the paint dry clay
then the old cry of warning—
Ko-ko-has Ko-ko-has Ko-ko-has
The blood-deep name of spruce smells,
the balsam touch firm underfoot,
soft as wingspread the feathered wind
drawn back, drawn back the ancient song
which is my brother's name.

Ko-ko-has Ko-ko-has Ko-ko-has Ko-ko-has
you waited in trees outside our village
you called to wake us when the pale Long Knives came.
The starlight glittered their metal of thunder
yet we had been drinking their bitter water
and we fell, our blood caught in their dreams.

The wolf Malsum, and Nolka, the deer,
walk beside our waters, my heartbeat stops there
at the wall of skin, the pain of cramped fist
trying to hold that bowstring tight
hearing a name called from sleepless nights
my footsteps echoing down oak halls
among young men who did not speak,
who could not sing the language of birds.

Ko-ko-has Ko-ko-has Ko-ko-has
my own steps fell open, walking forward
into the past forever memory.
I tied one hair to the roots of an ash tree.
They could hold my soul in that place
as surely as they did not hear
that call from a spirit world others still fear
Ko-ko-has, the protector of our dreams.

This Blessing

Barney Bush [SHAWNEE / CAYUGA]

for Ryan

Out in the blue shadows of the porch
a 3 a.m. quarter moon   the first
summer triad nearly done
I am who i am in this chilled night of
stars   and imagine the voices   of relatives
their flesh and blood melded with
Ohio River earth   i hear their whispers
clustered among the smokey road of
the Milky Way   I draw its breath
inside me and pray for the hour upon
us all

I am who i am   who i was made to be
though i have recreated myself a hundred
times over   one for each escape from
the tentacles of oppression   and each
time   i have smelled the fragrance of
broken earth   gathered a mussels shell for
the long sleep   for this oldest blood that
runs through our veins

Each night in this loneliness away from my
homeland   i thank the spirit of this
D'neh landscape   for its open door   dens'gdawah[1]
and the door to this house that
welcomes refugees from the American Dream
and the dark medicine of greed
self destruction   and the dark vanity that
mumbles with the voices of chaos

Each morning i face the sun   and pray its
giver of light to bless all the relatives
to bless all this homeland
all those caught between the razors of
men   and women
to bless this day
this moment.

---

[1]*D'neh* is what the Navajo people call themselves. *Dens'gdawah* is Shawnee for
"open door."

Cedar Swamp

Gogsigi / Carroll Arnett   [CHEROKEE]

Where all the good things
are.
          A redtail's nest
forty feet up the east side
of a white pine.
          The old,
old whitetail buck who's
hunted me these twelve
Novembers—he's not the same
one, nor am I.
          Chickadees
in their black caps, as
amiable as the bluejays
are belligerent, feed on
partridge berries.
          Hemlock
more than a hundred feet
tall, mutilated years ago
by some fool's hacking
a large X in its north bark,
a sapling long before Columbus
got lost.
          And how many
red squirrels chattering at
the west wind sifting through
tree tops.
          Snyder is right:
the woods have time.
          Nothing
can hurt me here.

Eagle Poem

Joy Harjo   [MUSCOGEE]

To pray you open your whole self
To sky, to earth, to sun, to moon
To one whole voice that is you.
And know there is more
That you can't see, can't hear,
Can't know except in moments
Steadily growing, and in languages
That aren't always sound but other
Circles of motion.
Like eagle that Sunday morning
Over Salt River. Circled in blue sky
In wind, swept our hearts clean
With sacred wings.
We see you, see ourselves and know
That we must take the utmost care
And kindness in all things.
Breathe in, knowing we are made of
All this, and breathe, knowing
We are truly blessed because we
Were born, and die soon within a
True circle of motion,
Like eagle rounding out the morning
Inside us.
We pray that it will be done
In beauty.
In beauty.

lines from a pariah notebook

Lance Henson   [CHEYENNE]

1.

yesterday a small path of sunlight on a porch
in turin
now so far from the agony of aloneness
there are circling birds above a wheat field
a wind moves among small blue flowers

lost in a graceless age
i cannot find my belongings
a spider web hangs
holding tiny drops of rain
above a river

darkness leans from itself
listening for the remnant of light
a crow flies past
in its claws

something stolen from a dream

2.

a bird watches my shadow
and sitting under a blurred leaf
i recall a floating mirror where your face
was melting into me

these are moments of terror where innocence
is held in exile
words broken and bruised lay
around the prophets

im trying to find a cigar in a dark rented room
flashing lights through the curtains
waking up in a rainstorm
outside the window it is a normal berlin morning

she turns to me telling me we are really in boston
i watch small flowers growing out of a mountain
remembering the scent of morning frost
in an oklahoma field

May 25, '95
Luxembourg

Naming the Animals

Linda Hogan   [CHICKASAW]

After the words that called legs, hands,
the body
of man out of clay and sleep,
after the forgotten voyages of his own dreaming,
the forgotten clay of his beginnings,
after nakedness and fear of something larger,
these he named; wolf, bear, other
as if they had not been there
before his words, had not
had other tongues and powers
or sung themselves into life
before him.

These he sent crawling into wilderness
he could not enter,
swimming into untamed water.
He could hear their voices at night
and tracks and breathing
at the fierce edge of forest
where all things know the names for themselves
and no man speaks them
or takes away their tongue.

His children would call us pigs.
I am a pig,
the child of pigs,
wild in this land
of their leavings,
drinking from water that burns
at the edge of a savage country
of law and order.
I am naked, I am old
before the speaking,
before any Adam's forgotten dream,
and there are no edges to the names,
no beginning, no end.
From somewhere I can't speak or tell,
my stolen powers
hold out their hands
and sing me through.

The Origins of Corn

Linda Hogan

This is the female corn.
This is the male.
These are the wild skirts flying
and here is the sweet dark daughter
that passed between those
who were currents of each other's love.
She sleeps
in milky sweetness. She is the stranger
that comes from a remote land, another time
where sky and earth are lovers always
for the first time each day,
where crops begin to stand
amid brown dry husks, to rise straight
and certain as old people with yellowed hair
who carry medicines,
the corn song,
the hot barefoot dance
that burns your feet
but you can't stop
trading gifts
with the land,
putting your love in the ground
so that after the long sleep of seeds
all things will grow
and the plants who climb into this world
will find it green and alive.

In the Cornfield

Rex Lee Jim   [NAVAJO]

suddenly
three persons come upon an old man
hoeing with a digging stick
in the middle of the wide cornfield.
quickly
he asks, who are you?
promptly
one of the three persons answers, I am me, who else?
the old man
slowly, but surely lifts his strawhat,
wipes the sweat off his forehead
on the back of his left hand.
and he looks at the young bilagaana man
with his wife behind him who is swollen with a child.
the old man's answer comes bursting forth
through the bulging stomach, and the woman feels
each kicking foot stretching her pain.
you say you are you, but I say, you are not here yet.
although you stand before me, I only see
your father your mother your grandmother your grandfather.
the sun catches the Navajo grin in action.
see that stomach, the old man teases,
"that one is mine."
I don't translate that, and he continues,
you are still there, there in the stomach.
I won't see you for a long time.
he looks up at the sun and then
his eyes scan his wide cornfield.
I am there, dancing in the breeze.
and just then cornstalks whistle in the breeze.
and out of the dancing stalks rides a young Navajo man,
riding a buckskin, wrangler jeans polishing
an already hard worn saddle,
a silver buckle flashing in the sun, with its
oval turquoise imitating the sky.
he strides off the horse and says,
I brought lunch for you, my father.
and the old man bellows with joy and delves into his food.

Sky Woman

Maurice Kenny   [MOHAWK]

In the night
I see her fall
sometimes
clutching vines
of ripe strawberries,
sometimes sweetgrass,
other times
seeds
which will sprout.
Always
loon or crane
fly with her.

1

I imagine her standing
by the cauldron stirring,
her naked flesh spattered
by bubbling corn mush.
Dogs come from the dark,
wolves, to lick her flesh.
Blood runs from wounds
the dogs have made
with their sharp tongues

She will mother me
for generations.
Her endurance ensures mine.

2

He pulled a great tree by its roots
from the sky earth
and left a gaping hole showing
the dark. Waters rumbled.
She was enticed to look deep
into the hole. She clutched
her abdomen, the child she carried,
and falls . . .
Water birds attend her . . . loon,
crane, mallard. Turtle stretched,
quakes, rises to surface dark waters
and awaits her passage.

3

She filled woods with trilliums, baneberry;
she gave hawk flight, thrush song,
and seeded cedar and sumac.
She flecked her hand in cold waters
and fish came to nibble fingertips.
All about her was wonder.
She brought grains to the fields
and deer to sweet meadows;
she touched maples
and juices ran down the trunks;
she looked back/up and rains
fell . . . she brought surprise.

All this her grandsons made,
and the face in the mountain rock,
river currents, deadly nightshade,
forests of elm, tamarack, birch, white pine;
the little spirits and the red people;
wolf and wolverine and bear.
She brought delight . . .
the greenness of things.

This her grandsons knew,
the birthed twins . . . Sapling and Flint:
she brought beauty under nourishing sun
and illumination of the moon
and stars over winds blowing
from all directions.

                    I'll look
                    tonight
                    for her to fall
                    again
                    from among stars
                    with strawberries
                    or sweetgrass
                    held tightly in her hands.

This Is No Movie of Noble Savages

Adrian C. Louis   [PAIUTE]

Born of trees
whose timeless atoms
carried on their savage
act of indolence
in annual assault of leaves
upon the earth
while their branches
felt up the sky
where the white man's God lives,
this paper
holding these petroglyphs
is neither apology nor legacy
but a wanted poster.

Now, dauntless before Dante's
nocturnal emissions
of visions of Hell
I curse God and weep
because some creeps crept
through the back window and carried
away my typewriter
while we were at the wake.
When I find them,
they will bleed broken English
from shattered mouths
and my fists
will sing songs of forgiveness,
unless of course
they're my in-laws.

Evening Near the Hoko River

Duane Niatum   [S'KLALLAM]

On the bank of this Klallam river, I am
at rest and fall to earth the way
birch leaves grow small and thin in music.
Like coast wind echoes from the sea,
faces of autumn emerge in orange
and gold and mauve. Crickets spring
moss-lined goodbyes on path,
sandbar and raccoon tracks.
Bear grass trampled down all summer
outshines the illegible animal ancestors
passing through the contrary mirrors of stars

Yellow tulips claim there is no other world
than this hill which is as active
as the memory of a lavender field
in another country of the imagination's,
especially the one I saw in the eye
of a snail, rainbow's daughter. The cold
dampness of twigs and cones frames
the creatures of metamorphosis,
not the song higher than the osprey gliding
from one current to another above the river.
Desire rises and falls in the air
like the swallows chasing insects into fireweed,
reverses direction and zips through
the canyon, home to seed and wing.

The moon in a violet fancy dance,
vagabond in any season, any mood and light,
flings souvenirs to the dream catchers
running for the river, swings a cape
over shoulders as she goes to sleep
in the monolithic hollows of the sea.
The white horses of this beauty
take a step or two or three,
become the river's hoof beats of the mountain;
from the ruby-throated sky a sparrow
drops from branch to branch
into the heart-line of larch.

Stones Speak of the Earthless Sky

Duane Niatum

Memory hasn't a chord of what the family lost.
For centuries village ancestors potlatched salmon's
return so we could dance on the water like bugs.

Today the stones quit asking not to betray
their ceremonies, our ears deaf to their winter
story of mountain, river, cormorant, red-flowering

currant. Our car tracks trample their children
who vanish down the street like moonlight
into gutters, our abbreviated hours.

Topaz stones brought us dream circles in order
to never forget where the earth's heart cracked,
our shadows became ant fodder; we laughed

like flies and drank the blood from mirrors.
Flint raised his arm to the hummingbird's
fragrances, healing our eyes, spiky as sea urchins.

We ground Flint to a machine that exploded
with roadkill floating in toxins.
From a cave, ancestor stones gave us the cells

of trout, madrona, butterfly, eagle and grizzly,
gave us our birth song born of the sea,
gave us eagle feathers for the sunrise dance.

We chose instead to shoot the spotted-owl
from its borderless clarity,
turn off life like a video, including ours.

After Lightning

Simon J. Ortiz   [ACOMA PUEBLO]

For all we know, we could be
already crystal motes, shattered
by swift and quick surging light.
We would never be certain if we
had a chance at all,
                          only settled
a vast moment later into dim shadow,
gradually blending into the prairie,
the low hills, the horizon ours now.

The moment before always too late.

Skins as Old Testament

Carter Revard   [OSAGE]

Wonder who first slid in
          to use another creature's skin
for staying warm—like bloody violation,
     a heresy almost,
          to crawl inside the deer's
     still-vivid presence there,
to take their lives from what had moved
          within, to eat delicious life
then spread its likeness over a sleeping
     and breathing self, musk-wrapped
               inside the wind,
          the rain,
               the sleet—
to roll up in a seal-skin self beneath
     a walrus heaven
          on which the sleet would rap and tap,
               to feel both feet
     grow warm even on ice
or in the snow—they must have thought
          the flame from tallow was like
such warmth from fur and hide—
     it must have been some kind
          of revelation when the life
came back into a freezing hand or foot
     after the fur went round its bareness, even more
when human bodies coupling in
     a bear's dark fur
          found winter's warmth and then
     its child
          within the woman
               came alive.

What the Eagle Fan Says

Carter Revard

*For the Voelkers,who gave the feathers; for the Besses, who
beaded them into the fan; and for all the Gourd Dancers.*

I strung dazzling thrones   of thunder beings
on a spiraling thread   of spinning flight,
beading dawn's blood   and blue of noon
to the gold and dark   of day's leaving,
circling with Sun   the soaring heaven
over turquoise eyes   of Earth below,
her silver veins,   her sable fur,
heard human relatives   hunting below
calling me down,   crying their need
that I bring them closer   to Wakonda's ways,[1]
and I turned from heaven   to help them then.
When the bullet came,   it caught my heart,
the hunter's hands   gave earth its blood,
loosed our light beings,   let us float
toward the sacred center   of song in the drum,
but fixed us first   firm in tree-heart
that green light-dancers   gave to men's knives,
ash-heart in hiding where   deer-heart had beat,
and a one-eyed serpent   with silver-straight head
strung tiny rattles   around white softness
in beaded harmonies   of blue and red—
lightly I move now   in a man's left hand,
above dancing feet   follow the sun
around old songs   soaring toward heaven
on human breath,   and I help them rise.

---

[1] *Wakonda* (also spelled *Wakontah*) is the Osage word referring to the Creator.
The eagle turns from heaven and sacrifices itself to bring man closer to Wakonda's
ways.

Durable Breath

John Smelcer   [CHEROKEE/AHTNA]

for Peter Kalifornsky

Outside my cabin window
I hear Raven's muffled caw rise from the river.

A lamp burns low upon my table,
the air is still in the silence of the room.

I think often of that night in your trailer at Nikiski,
of the old stories you shared with me—

Dena'ina Suk'dua
"That which is written on the people's tongues."

As a child you were beaten with a stick
for speaking your native tongue. My father,

born at Indian River,
does not know his mother's language.

Tonight, Kenaitze Indians gather
at a Russian Orthodox Church

to mourn in altered syllables among white-washed
crosses and tarnished silver ikons.

As I lean toward darkness,
it is your voice that lifts

Raven's wings above the riverbank,
his ancient syllables rising like an ochre tide.

To Those Who Matter

Roberta Hill Whiteman   [ONEIDA]

for the Oneida speakers and teachers

The sunlight in your heart hovers
in your smile when you share
your knowledge. Women and men
of intelligence and grace,
you created the spirit of this place.
How you have aided
my soul, that fluttering thing
that tries to launch across the haze,
that wants to flit
beyond the first green leaves
of life.

The moonlight in your heart
fills this city as it sleeps
and dreams. That moonlight knits our wounds
through the many ways you think
of others climbing
the hills behind you.
Cold Mountain said don't lose
the moment's happiness. The same
wind that woke him wakes us now.

The starlight in your heart twinkles
in Duck creek, glistens like dew
on early grass. It
helps the buds break as now
into a shock of green.
When we talk sometimes I see
one intense immense earth
wider than our words and more profound,
brilliant as a breath,
wearing your radiance.

"Tradition from Inside"

Roberta Hill Whiteman

for Bentley Spang

Pot thrown on a wheel
fingers squished inside
the crowded darkness
push clay's body out
and keep it smooth

Fingers can't separate
without the whole wedge
slipping off center
growing sloppy in its shape
ending in the bin

Fingers outside move by
pulling up and out
throwing off the slag
the space of sky around them
The potter holds the pressure equal
in both hands as clay becomes
more than the cold promise it
was seconds ago
I thought of fingers

pushing inside a mound
and taking shape
when you claimed Indian artists
create "tradition
from the inside"
So that's what we're doing

pressed close in this dark
reeling, believing the center
holds because we answer only to the potter
whose other brown hand
applies equal pressure
from beyond.

References

NOTE: The following list of references includes only those poems which appeared in previous publications.

"Song for Bringing a Child into the World" and "Song for the Dying" from Densmore, Frances. "Seminole Music." *Smithsonian Institution, Bureau of American Ethnology Bulletin,* no. 161 (1956).

"He-Hea Katzina Song," "Hymn of the Horse" and "Deer Song" from Curtis, Natalie. *The Indians' Book.* New York: Dover Publications, Inc., 1968.

"Song from the Mountain Chant" from Matthews, Washington. "Songs of the Navajo." *Land of Sunshine,* vol. 5. [n.p.], 1896.

"Song of the Earth" from Klah, Hasteen (as recorded by Mary C. Wheelright). *Navajo Creation Myth: The Story of Emergence.* Santa Fe: Museum of Navajo Ceremonial Art, 1942.

"Yaqui Song" from Densmore, Frances. "Yuman and Yaqui Music." *Smithsonian Institution, Bureau of American Ethnology Bulletin,* no. 110 (1932).

"Quail Song" and "Bear Song" from Russell, Frank. "The Pima Indians." *Eleventh Annual Report of the Bureau of American Anthology, 1889–90.* Washington, D.C.: Government Printing Office, 1903.

"Havasupai Medicine Song" from Hinton, Leanne, and Lucille J. Watahomigie. *Spirit Mountain: An Anthology of Yuman Story and Song.* Tucson: University of Arizona Press, 1984.

"Arapaho Ghost Dance Songs" and "Paiute Ghost Dance Song" from James Mooney. "The Ghost Dance Religion and the Sioux Outbreak of 1890." *Fourteenth Annual Report of the Bureau of American Ethnology, 1892–93.* Washington, D.C.: Government Printing Office, 1896.

"Luiseño Songs of the Seasons" from Goddard du Bois, Constance. "The Religion of the Luiseño Indians of Southern California." *University of California Publications in American Archeology and Ethnology,* vol. 8, no. 3 (1908–10).

"Six Dream Songs" from Demetracopoulou, D. "Wintu Songs." *Anthropos,* vol. XXX (1935).

"Two Newe Songs" from Crum, Steven J. *Po'i Pentum Tammen Kimmapeh / The Road on Which We Came.* Salt Lake City: University of Utah Press, 1994.

"Song" [Nootka] from Densmore, Frances. "Nootka and Quileute Music." *Smithsonian Institution, Bureau of American Ethnology Bulletin,* no. 124 (1939).

"Cradle Song" from Swanton, John R. (ed. Franz Boas). *Haida Songs, Publications of the American Ethnology Society,* vol. III, (1912).

"In the Valley" and "She Will Gather Roses" from Garfield, Viola E., *et al.,* eds. *The Tsimshian: Their Arts and Music* (Publications of the American Ethnological Society, XVIII). New York: The American Ethnology Society, 1950.

"Utitia'q's Song" from Boas, Franz. *Journal of American Folklore,* vol. 7 (1894).

"Dance Song" from Roberts, Helen H., and Diamond Jenness. "Songs of the Copper Eskimos." *Report of the Canadian Arctic Expedition,* vol. XIV (1913–18).

"Old Song of the Musk Ox People" from Rasmussen, Knud (trans. W. E. Calvert). "Intellectual Culture of the Copper Eskimos." *Report of the Fifth Thule Expedition, 1921–24,* vol. VII, no. 1 (1929).

"Delight in Nature" and "Ptarmigan" from Rasmussen, Knud. *Snyhettens Sange.* Copenhagen: Gyldendal, 1961.

"Two Heart Clan" from Big Eagle, Duane. *ONTHEBUS,* vol. I, no. 3, Fall (1989).

"Inside Osage" from Big Eagle, Duane. *Inside Osage.* September (1994).

"Eagle Poem" from Harjo, Joy. *In Mad Love and War.* Middletown, CT: Wesleyan University Press, 1990.

"Naming the Animals" and "The Origins of Corn" from Hogan, Linda. *The Book of Medicines.* Minneapolis: Coffee House, 1993.

"Sky Woman" from Kenny, Maurice (ed. Joseph Bruchac). *Returning the Gift.* Tucson: University of Arizona Press, 1993.

"This Is No Movie of Noble Savages," from Louis, Adrian C. *Among the Dog Eaters.* Albuquerque: West End Press, 1992.

"Evening Near the Hoko River" from Niatum, Duane. *Green Mountain Review,* vol. VI, no. 1, Winter/Spring (1993).

"Stones Speak of the Earthless Sky" from Niatum, Duane. *Amicus Journal,* vol. 14, no. 3, Fall (1992).

"What the Eagle Fan Says" from Revard, Carter. *An Eagle Nation.* Tucson: University of Arizona Press, 1993.